GH01246453

Park Stories: *The Regent's Park*
with Primrose Hill

Park Stories: The definite article
© Ali Smith 2009

ISBN: 978-0-9558761-5-8

Series Editor: Rowan Routh

Published by The Royal Parks
www.royalparks.org.uk

Production by Strange Attractor Press
BM SAP, London, WC1N 3XX, UK
www.strangeattractor.co.uk

Cover design: Ali Hutchinson

Park Stories devised by Rowan Routh

Ali Smith has asserted her moral right to be identified as the author of this work in accordance with the Copyright, Designs and Patents Act, 1988.

All rights reserved. No part of this publication may be reproduced in any form or by any means without the written permission of the publishers. A CIP catalogue record for this book is available from the British Library.

The Royal Parks gratefully acknowledges the financial support of Arts Council England.

Printed by Kennet Print, Devizes, UK on 100% post-consumer recycled Cyclus offset paper using vegetable-based inks.

The definite article

Ali Smith

THE
ROYAL
PARKS

The definite article

I stepped out of the city and into the park. It was as simple as that.

It was January, it was a foggy day in London town, I had got off the tube at Great Portland Street and come up and out into the dark of the day, I was on my way to an urgent meeting about funding. It was possible in the current climate that funding was going to be withdrawn so we were having to have an urgent meeting urgently to decide on the right kind of rhetoric. This would ensure the right developmental strategy which would in turn ensure that funding wouldn't conclude in this way at this time. I had come the whole way underground saying over and over in my head, urgent, ensure, feasibility, margin, assessment, management, rationalisation, developmental strategy, strategic development, current climate, project incentive, core values, shouldn't conclude, in this way, at this time. But it also had to be unthreatening, the language we were to use to ensure etc, so I went up the stairs repeating to myself the phrase not a problem not a problem not a problem, then stopped for a moment at the Tube exit because (ow) my eye was really hurting, out of nowhere I'd got something in my eye.

It made everything else disappear. I stopped and stood. I blinked. I felt about in one of my pockets, folded the edge of a kleenex into what felt like a point and ran it along the inside of my lower lid. I blinked again and looked to see. The something that had been in my eye was stuck now on the edge of the kleenex. It was tiny, and it might once have had legs, hard to tell now. Maybe its legs were still in my eye; the eye was still stinging a little, still running. Running.

Legs. Ha ha.

Urgent. Core values. Shouldn't conclude. The eye was still a bit sore. I tried focussing into the distance. What I saw was the edge of the park. Then I saw myself pressing the button on the pedestrian crossing. Then I was crossing the road anyway, between the fast-coming cars, before I changed my mind.

On the wide path on Avenue Gardens I dried a bit of bench with the kleenex I still had in my hand. I sat down and held my other hand over the sore eye. I could hear traffic, background, faded. When my eye stopped stinging, I'd go back.

But it was turning into one of the days in January that spring sends ahead of itself. The fog would burn off. It was burning off right now. It was clearing, I could see. There were magpies. There were pigeons. There were all sorts of birds, everywhere. When was the last time I had looked at a blackbird, or at a robin? When was the last time I had looked properly at anything? There were runners on the park's paths. There was a cordon of very young schoolchildren out on a trip in the middle of the day. There was a man whistling, walking along holding a can of Skol ahead of himself. He was holding the can like a compass. There was a man in a wheelchair, being wheeled by a boy. The boy looked very like him. There was a man with a camera on a tripod. He was filming a woman who'd stopped to feed a squirrel. There was a woman doing a sideways-stepping walking exercise. There were two joggers and a dog. The dog, keeping the pace beside them, looked full of happiness, and there were patterns everywhere, in the line of benches stretching towards and away from me, in the fountains and the stone urns, in the trees, in the died-back tidied beds of flowers, and that's when I remembered out of nowhere something I hadn't thought about in years, it's back when I'm twenty-five, we've been together for six

weeks, we've no money, it's my birthday and as a birthday
present you sit me down and blindfold me. You lead me
by the hand, blindfolded, out of the flat to where your old
Mini with the holes in its floor is parked. You guide me
into the car and then you drive me I have no idea where.
There's a strangeness in every noise. Everything I touch and
everything that touches me is so complex that all my senses
flare. How closed-in things are when we're in the car, and is
this what open actually means, when you get me out of it,
still blindfolded, and lead me up a steep path, into what feels
like somewhere whose openness will never end? At the top
of this steepness we stop. You take me by the shoulders and
turn me so that I'm facing something I can't see yet. You
wish me happy birthday. Then you take the blindfold off
me.

It's light, colour, it's the top of the hill. It's the city
itself I see under the huge sky.

It was one of the best birthday presents I'd ever
been given, I knew now so many birthdays on, twenty five
years later, a different person yet the same person, sitting in
the park in the future, one hand over one eye. Where were
you now? I wondered. What were you doing right now in
the world?

A bee passed me. It was quite a large bee, bright
yellow and black. A bee in January? Far too early in the year
for a bee to be out, it should be wintering, it would surely
die. I'd better go, I thought. I had a (not a problem) meeting
to chair, and as clear as day the thought came into my
head. I could follow that bee up Avenue Gardens. I could
turn left and go to the Rose Garden. I hadn't been to the
Rose Garden for years. There'd surely be some roses out,
regardless of January, and I could go and see the little statue
of Cupid with his arrows, was I remembering rightly, riding
on the back of a stone duck or a goose or something? Cupid,
with the tips of his arrows dipped in honey. And what was

that old poem, about Cupid getting stung by a bee and complaining to his mother, Venus, and her holding her sides laughing at him because of the stings his arrows give lovers, and him put out by a tiny bee? Cupid, in a bed of roses, no, Cupid, as he lay among, Roses by a bee got stung. It was years since I'd thought of that poem.

It was years since I'd thought about any poem.

I would go and look at the little statue to see if Cupid really was sitting on the back of a bird, or if I was just imagining it. When I'd done that I could go to the meeting.

Urgent. The word was a bit shaming when I thought about it. Not a problem. What did not a problem actually mean?

I would go to the Rose Garden. From there I would walk to the boating lake, then up past the sports pitches to the big fountain, and round by the zoo.

From there I'd go to the bottom of Primrose Hill, choose a path, any path, and follow it to the top.

That was all, the passing thought, the mere slant of the thought of all the different possible ways there are just to cross a park, and that did it, the morning shook its pelt, slipped its rein and did a sideways dash across Regent's Park – no, not just Regent's Park but *the* Regent's Park, *the* park, the definite article, the park that began as a forest whose sky was the tops of its trees, then the park of the left-handed King on horseback chasing the stag (and that's why the park is the lopsided shape it is, because Henry the Eighth was left-handed, so when he drew over the map of the Abbess's woods to mark the land he wanted *thus*, that's what his hand did, made a great curve there and a straight line there). The park of grazing smutty sheep (it's Henry James who called them smutty), the park of visions and assignations, fairs and ballads, footpads in their element, prostitutes in their ribbons. The park of the pretty girl out walking among the pretty flowers, taken suddenly and kissed hard on the mouth, *pray, alarm yourself not, Madame, you can now boast you've been kissed by Dick Turpin*. The park with the roofless theatre, *A Midsummer Night's Dream* in the midsummer air. The park where the crowds fed as much cake and biscuit as they could to Jumbo, The Biggest Elephant In the World, who'd been sold to America, in the hope it'd make him too heavy to be shipped across the Atlantic.

First it was Cromwell felling the trees for the Navy, *534 acres with 124 deer and 16,297 trees of oak, ash, elm, wite thorn and maple*. Then it was Nash, deciding what new trees to use, pairing the colours of different kinds of tree to suit his villas. Then they felled the trees all over again for the twentieth century wars. More than three hundred bombs changed the shape of the place in the 1940s. And now it's now. The park that began with the lords and the ladies in their carriages. The park that evolved, that learned to open its gates to everybody, to hold all the city's hundreds of languages, the city's efflorescence, in the one place. *Great forest of wooded glades*; the first written description we have of the Forest of Middlesex, which became the Great Chase, the Marrowbone, the Marybone, the Marylebone Pleasure Gardens, the Marylebone Park, the Regent's Park, where today, like any old day of the week, the day in the park curved itself off like a bird into the air over the seven thousand, five hundred trees, the laughable colours of duck, the black swans in the Rose Garden drinking the earlier drizzle off their own backs, all the people on their way to work who love to walk through the park, the young couple slowing their pace for their old slow dog on the Broad Walk, the man shouting at the woman cyclist and the cyclist giving him the perfectly reversed V sign over her shoulder, the magpies gathering in wait for feeding time over the zoo's walls, the Primrose Hill bookshop where stray leaves from the park blow in at the door all year round.

The day in the park, like any old day, took its usual bee-line, one never threatened by mere winter (which only makes the fountains more beautiful, the ice forming all down the sides of them), and one that always makes something of itself, like the honey the Regent's Park bees make of their visits to the lime trees in Avenue Gardens, or the honey that tastes of roses in the seasons when the Rose Garden proves good pickings for the bees. Amber Queen. English Miss. Wandering Minstrel. Sweet Dreams. Ingrid Bergman. Anna Ford. Mayor of Casterbridge. Old Yellow Scotch. There are hives all over the park where, right now, the bees would be crowding together to keep the temperature up, would be taking turns to be circled and warmed by all the other bees, would be tending to the year's future bees in their cells; there are beehives in good quiet places all over the park.

Look at that, nothing but a passing honeybee, the kind of nothing that has two sets of eyes, that makes a thousand flower-visits a day, a creature so clever that bees are already teaching themselves to combat the mites and diseases that have been killing them off so rapidly and so mysteriously (to humans at least) over the past few years. What's honey? A sweetener? Two pounds of honey equals a hundred thousand bee miles. The ancient Egyptians were the first to use it as an antiseptic, it's good on a burn, and it's not just good with a cough or a sore throat, it can help fight anthrax, diphtheria, cholera, MRSA, and when doctors transplant people's corneas the replacements are transported in honey.

Without bees? Nothing. Nothing pollinated. Hardly any fruit, almost no vegetables. All the food chains disrupted, from the human one down to the insect.

The beekeeper's got twenty eight hives in the park at the moment. He has no idea if they'll survive the winter. Last year in the park only five out of twenty colonies survived, and the year that followed was rough; a too-warm February, a too-cold spring, a too-wet summer; the bees needed supplementary feeding, and God knows what's to come. He began with imported New Zealand queens; they're pretty, bright yellow and black. He's worked at creating new colonies, new queens, in case of the same kind of bee loss as last year.

Urgent. Current climate. He works for no salary. You might say it's a labour of love. He makes a tiny profit on the honey he sells. Local feral bees are much blacker in colour. Last year he saw the yellow of the bees foraging in the roses by the café in the Inner Circle and he knew immediately they were Regent's Park's bees. The summer honey tasted, last year, of lime and somehow of passionfruit. Does light have a taste? Does the park have a taste? The late extraction honey last year was sweet, dark and powerful.

Could any place be more historied and less ghostly? Where's the ghost of the poet, Elizabeth Barrett, stealing the park's flowers to put in an envelope addressed to her fiancé, Robert, in Italy? Where are the ghosts of Percy Bysshe Shelley and Mary Shelley, sailing their paper boats on the pond? Where are the ghosts of the forty-odd people who went skating in January in 1867 and drowned in the lake when the ice gave way? Even them, cold and shivering, with the right to be a bit aggrieved, the right to hang about complaining for over a century, they're just not here. It's all open air. There's nothing dead and gone about it. Elizabeth Bowen, watching the swans in their *slow indignation*; and Richard Wagner standing at the lake throwing bread to the ducks; and Samuel Johnson causing a mini riot because it's too wet for the fireworks he's come to see; Charles Dickens, melancholy, a woman's been drowned in the canal; old George Bernard Shaw young again on the seat of a far-too-fast bike; Dodie Smith filling the park with the imaginary barks of dogs; Sylvia Plath, real as can be, hearing the hungry lion roar over the crib of her newborn child; then Ted Hughes, newly bereaved, the zoo-wolf howl in his ears; and Virginia Woolf herself, howling or furious or sad, doesn't matter which, walking and walking by the flower-beds till it cheers her up, leaves her happily *making up phrases.*

There's the woman who comes into the park at half past six in the morning and spends all the daylight hours leaving little mounds of cake and sunflower seeds (she always buys organic), in the same places so the wildlife will find it there when it comes looking.

There's the story of the man who, nearly two hundred years ago, bought four tiny birds from a sailor he met in the park. He put the birds in his pocket. When he got back to his lodgings he set the birds free. He watched them soar up over London.

Bet you any money, even if they'd been snared there in the first place, those birds flew straight back to the park.

'One entire Park, compleat in unity of character'. Endless stories, all crossing across each other, and mine tiny, negligent, quick as a blink, where nothing much happened except this: I stepped out of myself and into the park, I stepped off the pavement and into a place where there's never a conclusion, where regardless of wars, tragedies, losses, finds, the sting or the sweetness of what's gone in a life, or the preoccupations of any single time, any single being, on it goes, the open-air theatre of flowers, trees, birds, bees, the open vision at the heart of the old city.

In this way, at this time, nothing concluded.

In other words: in foggy London town the sun, shining everywhere. The meeting could wait. It did wait, while I sat on the bench in Avenue Gardens and thought about the poem where the god of love gets stung by a bee and his mother laughs at him, and about whether there were as many different kinds of rose in the Rose Garden as there were different languages spoken in the city of London, and about the day back then when a visit to the park gave me back my own senses.

I had no idea where you were today in the world. But I remembered, sitting there in the park, what it meant that our paths had crossed. I remembered, too, that old Mini you had and how its floor had rusted right through, and how we could look down and see the surface of the road pass so quickly beneath us that going at thirty miles per hour, twenty, ten, even something near walking-pace, pierced me every time with what it was that words like fast or slow or road or city meant.

Urgent. Core values.

When I got cold I walked across the park in the happy noise of blackbirds.

Then I went to the top of the hill and looked at the view. The city gathered round the park and rose out of itself as usual. I saw it all over again, as if for the first time.

Cupid, as he lay among
Roses, by a Bee was stung.
Whereupon in anger flying
To his Mother, said thus crying;
Help! O help! your Boy's a dying.
And why, my pretty Lad, said she?
Then blubbering replyed he,
A winged Snake has bitten me,
Which country people call a Bee.
At which she smil'd; then with her hairs
And kisses drying up his tears:
Alas! said she, my Wag! if this
Such a pernicious torment is:
Come, tel me then, how great's the smart
Of those, thou woundest with thy Dart!

from *Anacreon*, translated by Robert Herrick

Thanks to: Rowan Routh, Nick Biddle, and especially to Toby Mason,
the Regent's Park beekeeper.

The website dedicated to the many literary and musical references
there are to Regent's Park and Primrose Hill is cornucopic. Here's to its
forager, John Black.
Visit http://www.regentsparklit.org.uk

This story is dedicated to Mary Chadwick.